Why Coyote Stopped Imitating His Friends

CHARACTERS

Story Man

Story Woman

Raven

Coyote

Black Bear

Woodpecker

SETTING

A Native American campfire

Story Man: The night is dark and clear. The stars are shining. We are here to remember the old days and ways. We are here to share our stories.

Story Woman: Long before people from all over the world came to this land, Native Americans lived here.

Story Man: We lived in the forests and fields. So the animals were very close to us. We felt that animals were as important as people, and that they could talk. We thought animals had magic powers.

Story Woman: This story is about Coyote. He was a good hunter, swift and light on his feet. He was a handsome animal. But he was not happy as a coyote. He wanted to be just like his animal friends. He spent a lot of time and energy trying to imitate them.

Story Man: As our story begins, a hungry Coyote is going to the top of Blue Mountain to see his friend Raven.

Raven: Hello, my friend! Why do you look so tired and sad on this beautiful day?

Coyote: I'm hungry, Raven. I've been out for hours, but the hunting has not been good today.

Raven: I'll be happy to help! Let me get my bow and arrow.

Story Woman: Raven shot an arrow up into the air. It came down through his wing without harming him.

Story Man: Raven had magic powers. When his arrow hit the ground, there was a huge piece of buffalo meat at its tip.

Raven: Here, Coyote. There is plenty of buffalo meat to share between us.

Coyote: This is a fine piece of meat. But I must repay you. Will you come and visit me tomorrow?

Raven: Yes, Coyote, of course, I will be very pleased to come.

Story Man: The next day, Raven came down from Blue Mountain to visit Coyote.

Story Woman: Coyote had made a new bow and arrow that looked just the same as Raven's.

Coyote: Welcome, Raven! I will now serve you some tasty buffalo!

Story Man: Coyote was ready to shoot his arrow straight into the air.

Raven: Wait, Coyote, don't! My bow and arrow are magic, but yours are not! You'll hurt yourself!

Coyote: Nonsense! I can do whatever you can do. I am quite sure of it.

Story Man: Coyote shot the arrow into the air. It came straight down and scraped the edge of his foot before it hit the ground.

Story Woman: Coyote's arrow was not magic. There was no meat at the arrow's tip. There was only Coyote with a hurt foot.

Coyote: Ouch!

Raven: Oh, poor Coyote! Please, let me help you bandage your foot.

Coyote: Thank you, Raven. I'm afraid that I don't have any food for you now. I'm sorry.

Raven: Don't worry. Next time I come, you will have gone hunting in the usual way, and we'll enjoy some delicious buffalo together.

Coyote: But I'm not a magic hunter, like you.

Raven: No, but you're a fine, skilled hunter, so you don't need magic to get your food.

Story Man: Coyote promised to go hunting in the usual way before asking Raven to share food next time. But he still wished he had his friend's magic powers.

Story Woman: Soon, Coyote longed for the taste of persimmons.

Story Man: So he decided to climb Rich Mountain and visit Black Bear.

Coyote: Greetings, Black Bear! Might you have any of those juicy, delicious persimmons to eat?

Black Bear: Welcome, old friend! They are on the tree right now. I can shake some off for you.

Story Woman: Black Bear was very strong. He pushed hard against the thick tree trunk. In no time, the ripe fruit was all over the ground.

Coyote: This is a wonderful treat! Tomorrow you must visit me. I will serve you persimmons, too.

Story Man: Black Bear was puzzled. He didn't think his friend Coyote was big enough to shake fruit from a tree. But he agreed to visit the next day.

Story Woman: Coyote knew he wasn't as strong as Black Bear, but his mind was made up to do whatever his friend could do. Coyote cut down a small fruit tree. He took the leftover persimmons from the day before and tied them to the tree. Then, he dug a hole in the ground and stuck the tree's trunk into the hole.

Story Man: Coyote's fake persimmon tree was ready when Black Bear arrived at his lodge.

Coyote: Welcome, Black Bear! Would you like to taste some of my persimmons?

Black Bear: Yes indeed, thank you. They do look ripe and tasty, and I am very hungry.

Coyote: Let me just shake some fruit off this tree for you.

Story Woman: Coyote began bumping the tree with his head.

Story Man: He shook and he bumped and he shook some more.

Black Bear: Be careful! You're going to hurt yourself! Let me help you get that fruit, Coyote.

Coyote: Nonsense! I can do whatever you can do. I am quite sure of it.

Story Woman: So Coyote bumped the tree even harder. But the fruit was tied on very tightly. Before long, the tree fell on his head with a loud crash.

Story Man: Coyote got quite a bump on the head. And not a single persimmon came off the tree.

Black Bear: Sit down and rest, Coyote. That bump must be very painful.

Coyote: Yes, it does hurt. I feel a little dizzy, too.

Black Bear: Here, let me untie these persimmons for you. Whatever were you thinking? What a silly idea!

Coyote: Yes, maybe it was. I wanted to be strong, like you, but it didn't work.

Black Bear: I may be strong, Coyote, but you run much faster than I do. I can't be quick like you any more than you can be strong like me.

Story Woman: Coyote and Black Bear munched on the persimmons. And Coyote agreed to let his powerful friend shake the fruit trees from then on.

Story Man: But Coyote was still not happy with who he was.

Story Woman: Coyote was soon looking for food in the forest again. He came upon a tree, where he met Woodpecker.

Coyote: Hello! I'm Coyote. Who are you?

Woodpecker: I'm Woodpecker. Welcome, welcome, please join me in a bit of lunch.

Story Man: Coyote noticed that the bird had what looked like a bright red flame on his head.

Coyote: My friend, your head is on fire! Your home will burn up if you don't put it out!

Woodpecker: Don't worry. There is no fire. I've always had these marvelous red feathers on the top of my head. I was born with them.

Coyote: I see. Well, that brilliant red head does make you look very special. Very special indeed.

Story Woman: Woodpecker shared his food with Coyote. After they ate, Woodpecker agreed to visit Coyote at his home the next day.

Story Man: As Woodpecker came to the door of Coyote's lodge, he heard strange noises coming from inside.

Woodpecker: Hello? Coyote? Are you in there?

Story Woman: Coyote was waiting for the right moment to light a bunch of straw he had placed on his head. He planned to show Woodpecker that he looked special, too. As soon as he had the fire going, he opened the door to greet Woodpecker.

Coyote: Come in, come in! Welcome to my lodge!

Woodpecker: Coyote, what are you doing? Are you crazy? Your head is on fire! We need to douse the flames before you hurt yourself!

Coyote: Oh no, it's certainly nothing to worry about. I've always looked this way.

Woodpecker: No, you haven't. Your head was definitely not burning when we met yesterday.

Coyote: Nonsense! I look just the way you do. I am quite sure of it.

Story Man: The straw began burning the fur on top of Coyote's head.

Story Woman: And Coyote couldn't think clearly anymore. So Woodpecker took charge.

Woodpecker: Quick, Coyote! We must dunk your head in the river. Hurry, now!

Story Man: Luckily, Coyote lived next to a river. He only had to go a few steps to stick his head under the cool water.

Coyote: Thank you, Woodpecker. You were right. My head was on fire.

Woodpecker: Why would you do such a thing?

Coyote: Your red feathers are so wonderful. But my fur is a dull brown.

Woodpecker: But you are such a handsome animal, Coyote. Don't you realize it's much better to just be yourself?

Coyote: Yes, I believe I've finally learned that the hard way. And it's much easier, too. Just be yourself!

Story Man and **Story Woman:** And that is why Coyote stopped imitating his friends.

Story Man: Our story is at an end. Think about what you have learned from Coyote.

Story Woman: Share the story with others. This is our tradition.

The End